Oops!

First published in 2010
by Wayland

This paperback edition published in 2011 by Wayland

Text copyright © Jillian Powell
Illustration copyright © Amanda Gulliver

Wayland
338 Euston Road
London NW1 3BH

Wayland Australia
Level 17/207 Kent Street
Sydney, NSW 2000

Series Editor: Louise John
Editor: Katie Powell
Cover design: Paul Cherrill
Design: D.R.ink
Consultant: Shirley Bickler

A CIP catalogue record for this book is available from the British Library.

ISBN 9780750260633 (hbk)
ISBN 9780750260671 (pbk)

Printed in China

Oops!

Written by Jillian Powell
Illustrated by Amanda Gulliver

WAYLAND

Look!

Here we are running.

Look!

Here we are hopping.

Look!

Here we are jumping.

Look!

Here we are skipping.

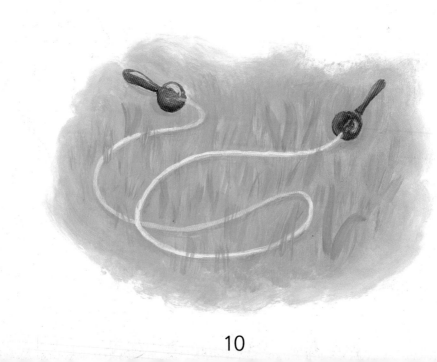

Look!

Here we are bouncing.

Look!

Here we are swimming.

Look!

Here we are climbing.

Look!

Here we are sliding...

Oops!

Guiding a First Read of
Oops!

It is important to talk through the book with the child before they read it alone. This prepares them for the way the story unfolds, and allows them to enjoy the pictures as you both talk naturally, using the language they will later encounter when reading. Read them the brief overview, and then follow the suggestions below:

1. Talking through the book
The two children in this book are doing all sorts of things outside. They want us to look at them.

The title of this book is Oops!
Let's look at the pictures on page 4.
The children say, "Look. Here we are running."
Turn to page 6. What do you think
they are saying here?
And what are they saying on page 8?

Continue through the book, guiding the discussion to fit the text as the child looks at the illustrations.

On page 18, the children are sliding.
So what do they say? Yes, "Look! Here we are sliding."
What do you think is going to happen on p20?
Turn the page. Were you right? Oops!

2. A first reading of the book

Ask the child to read the book independently, pointing carefully under each word (tracking), while thinking about the story. Praise attempts by the child to correct themselves, and prompt them to use their letter knowledge, the punctuation and check the meaning, for example:

You said, "Look! Here we are skipping."
Did your pointing fit? Try it again.
Well done, good pointing.

I like the way you checked carefully and changed your own reading. Why did you change it from 'swinging' to 'climbing'? Did you notice the 'c' at the beginning?

You made the story sound exciting. Well done!

3. Follow-up activities

The high frequency words in this title are:
are   here   look   we

- Select a new high frequency word, and ask the child to find it throughout the book. Discuss the shape of the letters and the letter sounds.
- To memorise the word, ask the child to write it in the air, then write it repeatedly on a whiteboard or on paper, leaving a space between each attempt.

4. Encourage

- Reading the book again — with expression.
- Drawing a picture based on the story.
- Writing one or two sentences using the practised words.

START READING is a series of highly enjoyable books for beginner readers. **The books have been carefully graded to match the Book Bands widely used in schools.** This enables readers to be sure they choose books that match their own reading ability.

Look out for the Band colour on the book in our Start Reading logo.

The Bands are:

Pink Band 1A & 1B

Red Band 2

Yellow Band 3

Blue Band 4

Green Band 5

Orange Band 6

Turquoise Band 7

Purple Band 8

Gold Band 9

START READING books can be read independently or shared with an adult. They promote the enjoyment of reading through satisfying stories supported by fun illustrations.

Jilllan Powell started writing stories when she was four years old. She has written many books for children, including stories about cats, dogs, scarecrows and ghosts. Jillian loves being outdoors, just like the children in Get Up and Go!

Amanda Gulliver always enjoyed art at school and went on to study Graphics and Illustration at College in Cornwall. Amanda now lives just a ten minute walk from the sea, where she can be found on the beach building sandcastles and collecting sea shells with her husband and two daughters.